PARADISE

A MICHAEL QUINN SHORT STORY

KEVIN SCOTT OLSON

D1444841

SPARTAN PRESS

Paradise

E*vening*
  The Central California Coast

IN THE DARKNESS, in the raging storm, the big eighteen-wheeler rounded the curve too fast.

Michael Quinn slowed his motorcycle as the truck's headlights appeared around the bend in front of him.

It looked bad. The desolate stretch of Pacific Coast Highway, with the sea on one side and rolling hills on the other, left the rig fully exposed to the elements. Waves of rain slammed the asphalt and rippled under the tires, turning the truck into a speeding forty-ton hockey puck.

The truck's black cab slid over the centerline, out of control. The cab turned back but the trailer jackknifed, dragging the entire vehicle across both lanes.

Quinn's heart pounded his ears as he pulled over to the guardrail at the seaward edge of the two-lane highway. He wiped the rain off his goggles and did the quick mental math of survival.

The truck was less than fifty yards away and headed right at him. He had three, maybe four seconds before it struck him broadside. The semi blocked the highway, and there was no time, on this flooded road, for the careful maneuvering required to turn the bike around.

To his right, past the guardrail, the cliff dropped straight to the sea. To his left, darkness hid what lay beyond the other side of the highway. If he shot across the road he might drive up a nice, easy slope. Or he might slam into the earthen equivalent of a brick wall.

Panic swelled in his gut as the mass of black metal loomed in front of him. For a split-second, he considered ditching his bike and leaping over the guardrail. But now there was no time even for that—the bike's headlight shone off the truck's glossy hood.

1

He turned his headlight to shine on the gap between the guardrail and the speeding truck. It was maybe two feet wide. But it was a chance.

The truck's horn blasted like a train and the rig was almost on top of him. The driver's startled face flashed pasty white through the windshield. The man was shouting something, his hands yanking the steering wheel.

Now. Quinn gunned the throttle.

The bike rocketed forward into the gap. The rear tire skidded, then held. Quinn's boot scraped the guardrail and the bike wobbled as he shot past a blur of rain and wet metal.

Then the open road lay in front of him and he was through. He swerved to a stop in the center of the highway and looked behind him.

Truck tires screeched and regained traction as the cab, inches from the guardrail, swung back toward the road. The trailer lurched sideways towards the sea, then straightened out and followed the cab to the safety of the inside lane.

The truck rounded a turn and vanished into the night. Pacific Coast Highway was once again a curving ribbon of darkness. The dull roar of the storm sounded in his ears.

For a moment Quinn sat there in the rain, catching his breath. Then he turned his bike back toward the open road and cruised slowly in the middle of the outside lane. His limbs shook from the near-death experience. Fistfuls of rain pelted him, and the handlebars twisted in the buffeting winds.

What had been so urgent that the driver chose to risk his life in this treacherous storm?

Perhaps the driver was behind schedule and worried about losing his job. Or amped on opioids. Maybe he was anxious to get to a date, to a woman impatiently waiting for him at a truck stop.

Quinn clenched his jaw as a gust of rain slammed his cheek. Those few seconds had almost been the end. Not in a blaze of glory. Not at the peaceful end of a long and fulfilling life. Random, aimless fate had come close to wrapping things up with an obscure highway accident, of interest only to the back pages of the local throwaway newspaper.

He passed a closed gas station, its old-fashioned circular pumps silhouetted in the darkness. This was a lone stretch of highway, without towns or streetlamps, nothing but finicky Mother Nature in a bad mood. It would be a cold and miserable three-hour ride home.

The bike droned through a series of S-curves, then something glimmered ahead. Turquoise light, flashing off and on, floating as if some ethereal specter. Probably the light bar of a California Highway Patrol car. The CHP car might have stopped next to an accident.

The glimmer vanished as he rounded a curve into a stretch of road so pitch-black he felt the queasiness of vertigo.

Another bend and the turquoise light reappeared, this time larger and hovering in the air to his left. It wasn't a CHP car. He wiped his goggles, and the blurry light cleared into a twenty-foot tall neon sign.

The top line flashed *Paradise* in turquoise script with a neon palm tree above the word. The white block letters below read *Motor Court* and below that *Visit the Paradise Lounge*.

He slowed and looked behind the flashing sign. Queen Palm trees fronted the property, their tall trunks bent in submission to the storm. Behind them the motel office and its attached Paradise Lounge were unpretentious, single-story buildings facing the highway. Lights beckoned from the Lounge.

Anything that got him out of the rain sounded promising. His leather jacket kept his upper body dry, but his jeans were soaked through. He'd packed a change of clothes and his shaving kit in his duffel bag. The storm would pass during the night, and he could cruise home in the morning sunshine.

Not to mention the fact he'd almost been splattered across the highway.

One does not tempt fate twice in the same night.

He pulled over under the arched stucco portico and killed the engine. His tired legs ached as he climbed off the bike.

TWENTY MINUTES *later*
The Paradise Lounge

· · ·

3

A HOT SHOWER, a change of clothes, and an ice-cold Negra Modelo made the world a friendlier place.

Quinn sat alone at the bar, his hand wrapped around the frosted bottle. He relaxed in his clean tee-shirt and jeans while the dark lager dissolved the road tension. On the muted television behind the bar, a pretty weather girl pointed to videos of mudslides and stranded motorists.

The décor of the Paradise Lounge stepped back decades in time. Knotty pine walls surrounded a well-preserved pool table and a dining area with wood tables and a handful of customers. Warmly lit with comfortable leather chairs, the humble room was a refuge from the rain pounding the roof and sheeting off the covered walkway.

The gray-haired, seventyish woman who'd served him lingered at the sink, washing glasses. She glanced at him.

"Can I get you anything else? Our kitchen is closed, but we have roast beef sandwiches."

"I'm fine, thank you, ma'am." Quinn sensed that she was the owner. He thought of the fifties-style décor and the old-fashioned coffeemaker and television console in his room. "Nice place you have here. Kind of a retro look?"

Her watery eyes shone with interest. "My guests have been using that word for some time now. My husband and I inherited this place from my parents, back in the seventies. We were newlyweds."

She set down the glass she'd been drying and picked up another. "He passed a couple of years later—cancer—and all of a sudden I was a widow in my twenties. Decided to keep everything as it was. There used to be other motor courts along this stretch of highway, one with a giant neon cowboy sign, another with a big wigwam. Now I'm the only one left."

What caused the curious tendency of some people to pour out their life stories to traveling strangers? He was about to reply when a chair scraped behind him.

"Checkmate!" pinged a youthful female voice.

He swiveled on his barstool. A young woman sat at a table for two with a chess board in front of her. She wore jeans and a Stanford sweatshirt. An elderly white-haired man dressed in rumpled slacks and shirt, and a well-worn brown sport coat, sat across from her.

"Professor, you can't play chess and work on your memoirs at the same time." The young woman looked up from her game and folded her arms in mock impatience. Her hair was tucked up in a visor. The visor tilted up, and Quinn glimpsed honey-brown eyes.

"I am quite capable of multi-tasking." The man glanced at the chessboard, then went back to writing on a yellow legal pad. "And your play was so slow I decided to let you win this one. Memoirs must be completed during one's lifetime."

Something about the man was familiar.

Quinn realized he was staring and glanced around the room. The only other customers were two elderly couples having dessert and, in a booth on the far side, four men in coveralls talking quietly over bottles of beer.

"You have plenty of time, professor." The girl put the chess pieces back, then stood. She stretched, looked around the room, wandered over to the pool table, and selected a cue from the rack.

"I'm bored. Do you know how to play this game?" Her fingers caressed the cue tip. She was petite, inches taller than the cue. The baggy sweatshirt and lack of makeup indicated the sort of busy college student not overly concerned about her appearance.

"I know a great deal about history, a fair amount about chess, but nothing about that particular endeavor." The man picked up his whiskey and turned his gaze to Quinn. "Perhaps this young man would be kind enough to show you."

That voice, the refined use of English.

"It would be my pleasure, Dr. Hartman." Quinn eased off his barstool.

"We have met?" White eyebrows arched in puzzlement.

Quinn walked over to the table. "Several years ago. You were a visiting professor when I was a graduate student at Oxford. Your class 'Freedom in the Twenty-First Century' was quite memorable. Michael Quinn, sir."

The professor rose to shake his hand. "Forgive me, I—wait. Yes. I remember you from the after-class sessions at that coffee house." A warm smile creased his face. "Please, have a seat."

Across the room, the girl rolled the cue ball down the middle of the pool table. Quinn felt her watching him.

Time had deepened the lines on his face and freckled it with age spots, but otherwise Dr. Hartman looked as Quinn remembered him. The angular features formed a kindly face. The lean torso showed little of the gravity-induced sagging that came with advanced age, and the snow-white hair revealed no signs of thinning.

Everything about Dr. Hartman's demeanor bespoke the civility of an Old-World academic. He sat in his chair in the patient manner he had in the coffee house discussion groups. When Quinn first saw him lecture at Oxford he assumed the professor's life had been the placid one of a scholar.

Until he learned who Dr. Benjamin Hartman was.

Quinn's mind was a jumble of memories as he sat down across from a man somewhere north of ninety years old. The clear gray eyes looked him over with polite curiosity.

"Mr. Quinn, if I recall, you attended Oxford as a Rhodes Scholar. Did you receive your Masters?" The voice had grown raspy but kept its cultivated manner.

"I did, sir."

"May I ask, in what field?"

"Politics and International Relations."

"An intriguing choice." Dr. Hartman's face lit up with interest. "I am interested in your thoughts on the world in these times, when parts of the globe are…" He paused for a drink of whiskey.

"On freaking fire?" Quinn sipped his beer.

"That does sum it up," replied Hartman drily. His lips pursed in a wry smile, and the eyes sparkled at the banter. "Where shall we begin?"

The conversation flowed as if they resumed a discussion begun in the Oxford coffeehouse. At times their talk was so lively they finished each other's thoughts. The pace would ebb when Hartman, using his beloved Socratic method of dialogue, posed a question designed to stimulate critical thinking, and then pick up again as soon as Quinn responded.

The girl watched them with amusement, rolling random balls so they banked off a gold diamond and into a pocket. After a few minutes, she shrugged, wandered back to their table, and waited expectantly.

Professor Hartman cleared his throat as they stood. "Rebekah Adler, please meet a former student, Mr. Michael Quinn."

Quinn grasped her extended hand. It felt delicate and feminine. He held it lightly, as he would hold a small bird. Beneath her visor, honey-brown eyes looked him over.

"Remember, you're going to show me how to play pool." She was still holding the cue.

"I promise, in a few minutes. Please join us." Quinn pulled a chair over from another table and they sat down.

Dr. Hartman swirled the ice in his glass of whiskey. "Rebekah is the granddaughter of an old friend. Her passion lies not with world events, but with mathematics. She is on her way to Stanford to start her Ph.D. program. As my travels also take me there, I have agreed to be her chaperone."

Rebekah patted the old man's arm. "Professor, you're too modest. Your trip to Stanford is also to receive a prestigious humanities award. Look, it's even made the news." She pointed to the television monitor on the wall behind the bar.

The local news showed video clips of the professor's career. Recent footage showed him speaking at the United Nations and before Congress, while a scroll at the bottom of the screen read: *"Dr. Benjamin Hartman, eminent historian, renowned Holocaust scholar, to be given Stanford University's famed Lifetime Achievement award...After receiving Nobel Prize ten years ago, Stanford award to cap professor's distinguished career...praised for his lifelong defense of freedom...ceremony to be attended by leaders from around the globe."*

The screen changed to a series of old black and white photographs. Some were engaging, and some were bleak, from one of the darker periods in history. The scroll read: *"Captured by Nazis while still a teenager...sent to death camp...Hartman led inmates in daring midnight escape from the Nazi concentration camp."* The montage ended with Hartman speaking a month earlier in Switzerland, with the scroll: *"Holocaust scholar warns that history repeats."*

The news anchor then showed a brief photo of the Lifetime Achievement award plaque. Quinn caught the words "enduring contribution to humanity" and then the screen cut to the weather girl, pointing to a live video feed from a shorted-out power station.

The picture flickered, and the restaurant lights dimmed as rain pummeled the shingled roof.

Rebekah sighed. "We were going to drive straight through but got waylaid by this stupid storm. Now we're stuck here for the night."

"There are far worse places." The professor shifted in his chair as the lights brightened. "Mr. Quinn, thinking of Rebekah reminds me that you were also a promising student. What direction has your career taken since Oxford?"

Quinn thought for a moment. "In a sense, it changed because of your class."

"How so?"

"Do you recall that late-night coffeehouse session when you recounted your escape from the Nazis?"

"I do."

"That evening became a turning point for me."

Rebekah leaned forward. "Oh! Professor, I've always wanted to hear the story of your escape from that Nazi death camp. My grandfather? I couldn't get two words from him about it. He would always change the conversation when it came up."

Hartman shook his head. "It is not a subject for conversation with a young lady."

"Professor, I'm twenty-one, not fourteen."

"It is not pretty."

"You've always urged me to take an interest in history, pretty or not. And tonight, with us cooped up in here seeking shelter from that horrible storm outside, you've got a captive audience." She leaned forward, imploring. "Please, Dr. Hartman, this evening was meant to be."

"Mr. Quinn, you have no objection to hearing it again?"

"To the contrary, sir, its lessons are timeless." Quinn glanced at Rebekah. 'And I agree with the young lady that this occasion, where our three paths have crossed in this out-of-the-way place, is fortuitous."

"Very well, then." Dr. Hartman's eyes closed for a few seconds, and when they opened they looked out the windows, at something far away.

Outside the storm raged on, unforgiving. Rain hammered the ground and clattered against the window glass. Yellow-white lightning arced somewhere over the mountains, followed by distant thunder.

The old man spoke in a matter-of-fact tone. "I was not yet sixteen when the invading Nazis rounded up everyone in my village and shipped us off to a concentration camp. You already know what most people know, from popular culture, of the cruelty of daily life in these Nazi camps, so I will avoid unnecessary detail."

His eyes narrowed. "What brought my life there to a flashpoint, however, was one particular guard. He was a member of the *Schutzstaffel*, the SS, and was sadistic beyond the norms of even his profession. He had a habit of coming into the prisoners' barracks at night and brutalizing the inmates. In the barracks, he would perform mock inspections, boasting that he had the power to torture and kill any of us at will if he found an infraction.

"There was this ring on his finger, a ring with a death's head insignia on it. He bragged that the ring meant that he was in the elite *Einsatzgruppen*, which massacred entire villages of civilians in Poland. Some they tortured and shot, some they burned alive in their homes. So proud of that, he was! He would grin and tell us that executions had become a pleasure sport for him."

Quinn's grip tightened on his beer bottle. Once, in class, the professor had rolled up his shirt sleeve and showed the numbered tattoo on his forearm to shocked students.

The professor continued. "Then, to prove his point, this SS guard would find an infraction, choose an inmate at random, and pistol-whip him.

"The other inmates knew to keep quiet. Ah, but I was young and headstrong. One night, I lost it. I was shaking mad, and I yelled and cursed at this man."

Dr. Hartman looked down at the amber liquid in his glass. "He walked up to me, shoved me, and said I was finished. He brought his face up close and said that to make an example of me, the punishment would not be pistol-whipping. It would be execution by hanging. He spat at my feet and left."

"What a monster…" Rebekah spoke the words softly, almost to herself.

Hartman sighed. "I lay in bed that night, scared and angry at my foolishness. Then I realized I was going to die in that camp if I didn't escape. It was time for action.

"The next evening that SS guard barged into the barracks, later than usual. We were all in bed. He stank of alcohol, and when he yelled and cursed his words slurred. My bunk was towards the back, and he picked a prisoner near the front for that night's taunting and beating."

Dr. Hartman sipped his whiskey, re-living the night.

"I had my clothes on under my sheet. On the floor beneath my bunk was a twenty-pound sledgehammer I had pilfered from work. When he bent over to pistol-whip the prisoner, I ran up behind the guard and, with all of my strength, swung the sledgehammer into the back of his head.

"The force of the blow crushed the man's skull, and he crumpled to the ground, dead. I had been frightened, but at that moment my mind cleared. Now there was no turning back. Moving quickly, I relieved the guard of his P08 Luger and spare magazine, then I shoved his body under a bed."

Rebekah caught her breath as a shudder rippled through her upper body. Quinn touched her arm, and she nodded that she was okay. The professor glanced at her, then he continued.

"I had a weapon, but I needed a distraction to occupy the other guards on night duty before we could make our escape. I told the other prisoners to be ready and wait for my shout.

"I slipped out of the barracks, keeping low to the ground, and ran to the motor pool in a back corner of the camp. There was a massive gasoline tank there, and several fifty-gallon drums. I opened a drum of gasoline and poured its contents under the tank, rolling it backward to make a trail of fuel. I lit the fuel with a cigarette lighter, and with a *whoosh*, the tank was surrounded by leaping flames. Then I took the guard's Luger and fired it at the tank."

Hartman glanced down at his hand, curled around his glass. The hand that had once held the Luger was now gnarled and speckled with age spots. "It took a few rounds, but the resulting explosion was so massive, it set adjacent buildings and vehicles on fire. It even knocked out part of the camp's electricity. As I sprinted back past the barracks, I yelled, and my fellow prisoners poured out."

Dr. Hartman gazed out the window at the storm, whose unrelenting downpour surrounded the Paradise. The rain pounding the roof and the winds howling all around seemed purposeful, as if trying to break in.

"It was winter and bitterly cold. We ran for our lives toward a section of the boundary fence in darkness from the electrical outage. In the distance, we could hear the guards yelling to each other.

"When we reached the barbed-wire fence, guards shouted orders to send out a search party. They had found our empty barracks. I had a pair of wire-cutters and cut through the barbed wire. Since it was my escape plan, I felt responsible. I decided to stay until all of the prisoners made it through.

"About half of them were through the fence when the searchlights from the watchtowers clicked on. Alarms sounded and sprays of machine gun fire from the towers blasted the ground closer and closer. But by the time the searchlights found the opening in the fence, we had all made it into the surrounding forest."

Dr. Hartman finished the last of his whiskey. "The Nazis launched a massive manhunt, but we kept going. We ran for miles and eluded them. Fortunately, we found friendly villages and, in brief, dispersed until after the war." He set his empty glass on the table with a soft *chink*.

Rebekah had been sitting hunched forward with her arms on her knees, listening intently. She exhaled and leaned back in her chair. "Such horrible times. It's hard to believe they really happened."

"They did," replied Hartman.

"We are fortunate, then, to live in this modern age. Such barbarities are obsolete and will never happen again." Rebekah picked up the pool cue. "That is why my interests do not lie with the past. They lie with the future."

Quinn looked at her. "Ignorance of the past can be dangerous. It can lead to indifference about the future."

Hartman looked at them both. "And indifference can lead to oblivion."

The girl opened her mouth to reply but gasped as lightning flashed outside the Paradise. Huge jagged bolts streaked from sky to earth, followed by a thunderclap so loud the ground trembled beneath them. Rain crashed against the windows like buckshot. The table was silent as they listened to the thunder recede and the storm return to its somber roar.

Rebekah regained her composure and tapped the cue in her hand. "Professor, thank you for the moving story. Now I believe I am owed a pool lesson."

Dr. Hartman smiled and ran a hand through his hair. "Please forgive the impertinence of the young lady. She is a free spirit." He looked at Quinn.

11

"Before you go, young man, I am curious to hear about that turning point of yours."

Quinn put his beer bottle on the table. "Yes, of course. Well, when I started graduate school, I had plans for a business or academic career. But after that night at the coffeehouse, with all that was going on in the world, I realized that diplomacy and negotiating can only go so far.

"There are times when action is called for. When a warlord threatens your survival, the only thing that will get his attention is a warrior."

He looked at the professor. "At Oxford, there is a stone wall engraved with the names of the Rhodes Scholars who served in the two World Wars. I felt an obligation to serve my country as well and served six years as a Navy SEAL."

"Well done." Hartman nodded. "But I notice the past tense. Your service since then?"

Everyone at the table was silent for a moment. Hartman's eyes widened. "Of course! You are not at liberty to discuss your current activities. I understand."

The girl, a look of polite boredom crossing her face, pushed her chair back. "And I understand we have had enough history for one night." She stood and brandished her pool cue. "Now it is time for this new game." She put her hand on Quinn's shoulder and let her fingers drift down to his bicep.

Hartman sighed as he put his legal pad in a battered leather briefcase. "Very well, Rebekah. I am tired anyway, and ready for bed. I will leave your billiards instruction to the hands of this capable young man. But you will be in the cabin no later than eleven-thirty."

"Of course."

Dr. Hartman braced himself as he got up from the table and extended his hand. "Mr. Quinn, I hope our paths cross again." The gray eyes focused to take a mental photo, as if at his age, any encounter might be his last.

"Looking forward to it, sir." Quinn shook the firm grip and stood as the old man, slightly stooped, picked up a mahogany cane and made his way out of the lounge.

Fifteen minutes later, an excited Rebekah had grasped the basics of pool. Quinn used the diamonds to execute a simple bank shot, and she clapped her hands and laughed, "It's basic geometry!" A few minutes later she gasped when, showing off, Quinn managed to pull off a Masse' shot and make the cue ball reverse direction.

Quinn had been put off by her brash attitude towards Dr. Hartman. Now, he decided, he'd been too censorious. Her playful love of learning showed that her outgoing nature was her *joie de vivre,* and he found her engaging.

"Michael, if I want the proper angle to bank the yellow ball into the corner pocket, should I aim just to the right of that third diamond?"

"Yes. I can see your passion for math."

"Where else can you find a perfect world?" She watched as the yellow ball banked off the rail and rolled directly into the center of the corner pocket. "With mathematics, there's only one correct answer. You can attain absolute truth! In the liberal arts—history, philosophy, all of it—no one can agree on anything. What good is that?"

"What will you be working on at Stanford?"

"The Riemann Hypothesis. One of the great unresolved—ah, we can talk about that later." Her eyes met his. "I, Rebekah, hereby challenge you, Michael, to my first game of pool. My superior knowledge of geometry versus your skill sets." She removed her visor and looked at him with mock seriousness that dissolved into a grin. "An even match. But can you get me one of those cold beers first? It's getting warm in here. They must've turned the heat up." She turned around and began pulling her sweatshirt over her head.

Quinn walked to the bar and ordered drinks. The owner chatted him up, curious about the presence of such a celebrity. How well did he know the professor? Was that college girl famous as well? When he turned around with the two cold Negra Modelos, he took one step toward the pool table and halted.

The frumpy grad student had vanished. Quinn watched as Rebekah removed a hairbrush from her purse, leaned back and brushed thick, brown hair that hung to the waist of a very attractive woman.

Arching her back displayed a figure as slim and beautiful as that of a ballerina. Twin curves of milk-white breasts peeked from her low-cut tank top. Her flimsy top didn't quite reach to her low-cut jeans, revealing a tantalizing glimpse of a firm white waist.

She put her brush away, gave her hair a final shake, and smiled at him as she posed next to the pool table like a calendar girl.

"Michael, do I need to, what do you call it, break?"

"Yes, that's how you start. This is about the only time you'll want to put your body into it and hit the ball hard." Quinn walked over with the drinks and put them on a table.

"Can you show me?" She held out the pool cue and stood next to him, her gaze catching his. Up close and with the visor gone, her face was striking. Dark eyebrows arched high above her eyes, and below her delicate nose, her pouty lips were full. Her skin was flawless and almost the color of alabaster, befitting someone whose interests were cerebral and indoors.

Quinn put his arms around her taut waist and held her hands around the cue stick. The lemon fragrance of body wash or perfume teased his senses.

"Now!" He squeezed her hands and rammed the cue stick forward.

Rebekah squealed as the balls broke in a circle, and a striped ball rolled into the corner pocket. "Does that mean I'm stripes?"

"Yes, and you keep going. Now, if you hit the cue ball softly on the right side, you can knock those balls touching each other into the pocket. Hold the cue like this." Quinn stood behind her, wrapped his arms around her waist again and set her position. The lemon fragrance was intoxicating. As she leaned forward her cotton top rode farther up, exposing the pale small of her back and the even whiter curves of her posterior. Her soft skin brushed against him as she bent over and, after a deep breath, pushed the cue stick forward.

The cue ball spun smoothly on its axis and seemed to glide across the felt until it gently struck its target. One after the other, the two striped balls rolled languidly into the pocket.

"Yes!" Rebekah pumped her fist. She turned toward Quinn and, without warning, gave him a hug and a peck on the cheek.

Quinn mumbled, "Awesome." He gently put her arms back at her sides and stepped back, assessing the situation.

What was with the PDA? Could be just her natural exuberance. Some women were like that. Surely, she knew he was her *de facto* chaperone until she went to bed? That nothing was happening tonight?

Was it?

His body still tingled from her hug and kiss.

He glanced around the room. The elderly couples were at the register, paying their checks while making small talk with the owner. The men in coveralls lingered over their beers.

The rain on the roof reminded him that a couple of hours ago he'd been resigned to a cold and dangerous ride home. Now he was warm, dry, and savoring a Negra Modelo. A chance encounter had reunited him with a treasured mentor from his past. And he had made a new friend.

Paradise did not have to be complicated.

Rebekah tossed her hair back as she bent over and practiced her next shot. Her curves were prominent in the skinny jeans and cotton tank top.

Behind them, someone cleared his throat.

Quinn spun around, startled to see the four men in coveralls. He hadn't heard them get up. They stood a few feet away, facing him.

One stood in front, the other three grouped behind him. Their silence, rather than respectful, was hostile.

Quinn's instincts kicked in and he stepped forward, putting himself between Rebekah and the men, and assumed a balanced stance. Keep it civil. "What's up?"

"We're gonna shoot pool now. That's what's up." The apparent leader, a man with a shaved head and a scraggly chin beard, stared at him. Taller than the others at about six-foot-three with a wrestler's build, he flexed powerful arms.

Quinn held the pool cue in front of him as he looked the men over.

The four men wore gray coveralls with "Coast Cities Auto Repair" embroidered in black. None wore name-tags. The Alpha-male leader, with the chin-beard, had pale skin like an albino, but with a pallid, sickly-looking hue. Beads of sweat ringed his forehead and upper lip. His eyes were a yellowish-brown color that reminded Quinn of jaundice. He leered at the girl.

The yellowish eyes flicked back to Quinn, awaiting an answer.

"We're in the middle of a game." Quinn, mindful of the girl, kept his tone unchanged. "You can have the table when we're done."

Adrenaline coursed through Quinn's veins as he spoke. The situation in the lounge had, in seconds, taken a one-eighty. The mellow vibe evaporated, replaced by tension snaking through the room like invisible fog. The body language of the four men—aggressive posturing and aggravated expressions—revealed everything he needed to know.

They were the only ones left in the room. The owner had gone through the kitchen's double doors, probably to close the motel office.

One of the other men in coveralls stepped forward. Shorter, with greasy black hair, he had the fit, wiry build of a tough street fighter. He pointed a finger at Quinn, displaying a forearm tattoo of the Grim Reaper. His voice was higher-pitched. "You don't own this joint, mister. You've had the table for a while. We're done eatin' and want to get in a few games before the old lady closes the place. You got a problem with that?"

Behind him slouched a lanky man with skull tattoos on his forearms and dirty brown hair sticking from beneath his baseball cap. Next to him stood the fourth man, pale and nervous-looking, with the furtive eyes of an addict. He used a finger to clean food off his gums, revealing the discolored, rotting teeth of a meth user.

Alpha, Street, Baseball-Cap, Meth. All had ex-con written all over them. Alpha had the height and reach, and looked like a brawler with a deadly punch. Street's likely speed and agility made him potentially even more dangerous. The other two were harder to gauge, but four against one was never good odds.

"You can have the table when we're done." Quinn kept his voice calm. "There's no need for trouble."

Alpha's expression darkened. This was a man not used to being challenged. He licked the sweat off of his upper lip. The jaundiced eyes turned opaque.

Then the eyes flared and Alpha brought his arms up at his sides, gesturing to the men behind him.

Street, Meth, and Baseball Cap fanned out. Heads tilted back or to the side, and they shot Quinn various forms of stare-downs. Street edged further to the side, out-flanking Quinn on the left.

Alpha jabbed a finger at Quinn. "You're leaving now, man. But she gets to stay. She wants to learn how to play pool, right? She can play with us."

"Yeah, let the little lady here have some fun." Street's voice rose a notch. As he spoke he inched closer to her.

Baseball Cap moved toward her from the other side, outflanking Quinn on the right.

Alpha brought his hands up in a ready position, moving in like a boxer with a cornered opponent. The yellowish eyes taunted. "Hear that, man? You ain't in charge here, so get the hell back to your room an' leave us alone. We just invited the lady to party. An' I didn't hear her say no."

Street stepped closer to the girl, forcing Quinn to glance his way.

Alpha's right hand darted forward, reaching for Quinn's t-shirt. At the same time, Street reached for Rebekah. His other hand grabbed his crotch. "Hey sweet-cheeks, ya want some of thi—"

The word hung in mid-air as Quinn whipped the pool cue around and knocked Alpha's hand away, then pivoted and rammed the cue tip into Street's gut. Street doubled over, the wind knocked out of him.

Alpha yelped in pain and drew his hand back. Street, still doubled over, squealed as Quinn brought his elbow up into Street's nose. Street staggered back and fell to the floor, his hands covering his face.

A whooshing sound from behind signaled Baseball Cap lunging toward Quinn, his beer bottle swinging at Quinn's head.

Quinn's right leg shot out. The low sweep kick caught Baseball Cap behind the ankle just before his foot hit the ground. Baseball Cap's leg went up, and as he fell backward, Quinn turned and rammed the pool cue into his chest.

Baseball Cap hit the floor hard on his back. His hands went limp and the beer bottle rolled away. Quinn stood over him and pressed the tip of the pool cue into the dip of skin between the man's neck and collarbone. Baseball Cap coughed and made choking noises.

Alpha took a step forward and stopped, rubbing the red welts on his wrist. Meth was frozen in place. Street sat on the floor with a dazed expression, dabbing at the blood running down his lips and chin and staring at his bloody fingers.

Quinn caught Alpha's eye and pointed to the prone Baseball Cap. "This man's in serious pain right now." He pressed harder on the cue.

Baseball Cap gasped for breath. His eyes widened.

"The cue is pressing on his jugular notch," Quinn continued. "Probably no permanent damage has been done, yet."

Quinn ratcheted up the pressure on the cue stick. Baseball Cap's chest shuddered and he made retching noises.

The temptation to finish off Baseball Cap and quickly take out the others flashed through Quinn's mind. But that would be messy and involve the authorities.

He caught Alpha's eye. "Here's the deal, badass. Clear your guys out of here, now. Or I crush your buddy's windpipe."

Alpha blinked. In a heartbeat, his demeanor changed. He seemed preoccupied, as if this incident was already in the past. "Okay, okay. No trouble, we're leaving. C'mon guys, we're outta here. Go!" he barked the order, still rubbing his wrist.

Quinn was taken aback by the quick surrender. He'd expected some trash-talk, a modicum of face-saving defiance. He stepped away and watched as Street wiped his bloody hands on his jeans and got to his feet. Baseball Cap rolled over on his stomach, got to his knees, and stood, one hand holding his throat.

Alpha motioned to the others and strode out the door, avoiding eye contact. Meth followed him, then the limping Baseball Cap.

Street stopped just before the doorway. He licked blood from his upper lip and glared at the girl. "We'll save you for later," he rasped.

He turned and closed the door behind him.

THE PARADISE MOTOR COURT was laid out in the low-rise architecture from the days of inexpensive land. Behind the motel office and lounge, a covered walkway led past a swimming pool to a common area of grass and gravel, and then to the cabins, which were arranged in a long U-shape, facing each other.

Rain formed a silvery curtain as Quinn walked a pensive Rebekah along the covered walkway. The chilly night air was a relief from the sweat and tension of the lounge.

She moved closer. "Thank you for protecting me back there. Who were those men?"

"Just lowlifes. A type you will want to avoid."

"I hope so." Her voice faltered as their footsteps crunched the gravel.

"Forget about them. Tomorrow morning they'll be gone, and you'll have a leisurely drive up the coast."

"Sounds good. Now tell me, Michael, who are you?"

"A friend."

"No, I mean who are you really? I've never seen anything like what you did."

"I'm just a friend." He stopped at the end of the covered walkway. "Put your sweatshirt hood on and I'll jog with you over to your cabin. Here, hold my hand. Ready, go!"

She giggled as they splashed through the puddles, and seemed more like her previous self when they reached her cabin door.

"Well, thank you again, whoever you are, for teaching me pool and—everything." She pulled her hood off and faced him. She was panting from the jog and leaned toward him, her lips parted.

Quinn gave her a peck on the forehead. He liked her, but he wouldn't be seeing her again. He glanced out at the cabins. They were all identical, with a pitched roof, a window next to the front door, and a window on one side. "I'm in cabin number twelve, over there, just across the way from you. Let me know if you need anything. Lock your door. Good night."

"Good night, Michael."

———

Thirty minutes later

Rainfall usually served as a sedative for Quinn, its rhythmic patter lulling him to sleep. Tonight was different. He tossed and turned and punched his pillow, trying to find the right position. He lay on his side and looked around the small room, at the couch across from his bed and the hotplate and coffeemaker on a table next to the tiny bathroom. Finally, he lay on his back and stared at the acoustic ceiling, listening to the rain drum on the shingles.

Maybe it was the severity of this storm which kept him awake. Or maybe it was the odd sense of unfinished business from the Paradise Lounge.

We'll save you for later.

What the hell was that about?

And there was more. Alpha had backed off too quickly in the lounge. This was something beyond the behavior of the typical sociopath. It was an I-know-something-you-don't arrogance, and it was disturbing.

He picked up his cell phone and surfed the net. With the remote area and the storm, the green signal-strength bars maxed at a shaky three out of five. Websites were slow to appear and quick to drop out. He typed in a search for Coast Cities Auto Repair.

His jaw tightened when a group photo of the four men opened on the business website. Their smiles looked as phony as a day is long. But the website looked legitimate, down to the testimonials. Their company van had been one of the few vehicles in the parking lot. Their cabin was down at the far end of the U-shape, away from Rebekah's.

We'll save you for later. An empty threat from a drunk. His fingers punched in a phone number.

"Michael, you realize it's after two a.m. here on the east coast?"

"If you have a date, Will, tell her this won't take long. Need a quick search."

"I was sleeping, dammit. And where the hell are you? My GPS is tracking you in the middle of nowhere."

Quinn summarized his whereabouts, the evening, and his run-in with Coast Cities Auto Repair. "My gut says something is up with these guys."

"Do you have names? I've got their website up."

"No."

"We'll try facial rec software. The algorithms on our latest version are damn good, especially with full-frontal headshots like these. Call you in twenty."

Quinn killed time doing a search for Dr. Hartman. Links to articles from the New York Times and the Jerusalem Post appeared, and a biography on his author page listed his academic achievements, books and articles, and numerous awards.

A search for Rebekah Adler returned several namesakes. He narrowed the search by adding "mathematics" and there she was, all over social media. Her favorite game was chess, she had just read a great biography of someone named Hilbert, and her Facebook home page picture was a color photo of her on a white-sand beach on a sunny day, emerging from calm ocean shallows, her body dripping wet in a turquoise bikini. She was, from head to toe, a natural beauty.

He was enlarging the photo when his phone vibrated.

"Michael, your gut was right. All of these guys are felons who did hard time."

"Gang-bangers?"

"Not that I can see. Those tattoos are standard prison stuff, no gang affiliation. They all managed to offend society in separate ways. In fact, it looks like they led separate lives until they met up in vocational auto shop class in Folsom."

Will's tone sharpened. "The big guy, your Alpha leader, convicted on two counts of voluntary manslaughter. The one with the bad teeth, a long string of burglaries. The tall one with the baseball cap, armed robbery plus aggravated assault.

"And the one who made a pass at the girl? He's a piece of work. A serial rapist. Four arrests, two convictions, the other two times the women disappeared and never showed up to testify."

"How long have these guys been out of prison?"

"One to two years. And they've stayed clean since. Not so much as a parking ticket. They could have gone legit, you know."

"Will, stop channeling your inner social worker. Let's dig deeper. I think there's more. Start with the leader, the big guy."

"You got it. I'm wide-awake now, anyway. And if I find anything, it'll give me the pleasure of waking you up."

Quinn laid his phone on the nightstand and stared at the ceiling. He had done his due diligence. There was, in all probability, nothing there. In the morning, Rebekah would move on to Stanford, and he would enjoy a leisurely ride home with the sun on his back. He took deep breaths, letting his thoughts drift back to Rebekah's soft skin in that turquoise bikini.

Slumber clouds circled his consciousness. He was drifting off when someone knocked on his door.

A petite figure in a hooded poncho peeked in his window. The poncho's hood hid most of her face, but in the porch-light, he recognized her fair skin and full lips. He rolled out of bed and opened the door.

"Rebekah, what is it?" He scanned the surrounding darkness. She was alone. The porch light to her cabin was on, but the other porch lights were dark.

"I'm sorry to intrude, Michael, but I can't sleep. Dr. Hartman snores terribly, and we have two twin beds in one tiny room. I left him a note with your cabin number in case he wakes up. And frankly, I feel safer here with you. May I sleep here?" She glanced at his room. "I'll be fine on that couch. I won't be any trouble. And I promise to be gone first thing in the morning. Please?" Strands of her hair blew in the wind as raindrops pelted her cheek.

"I can give you some sleeping—" He stopped mid-sentence. The rap sheets of the men stuck in his mind, with a red light flashing at Street's multiple rape convictions.

The girl *was* safer here with him. Sending her back now bordered on negligence.

"Of course. I'll get you a blanket and pillow." He opened the door and let her in, then locked it behind her and turned out the porch light.

The musty smell of wet poncho and hair filled the small room.

"I really, really appreciate this." The girl flipped the hood back and smiled as she shook the rain out of her hair. Quinn unwrapped the plastic-covered spare blanket and pillow that lay at the foot of his bed. He was sprayed by raindrops as she lifted the poncho over her head.

"It feels so good to get out of this wet thing." Underneath the poncho she wore nothing but flip-flops, pink ladies' boxer shorts, and a white cotton tank top.

Inches away, her figure was revealed in exquisite detail, far beyond the glimpses allowed in the lounge. Her skin shone a soft pearl in the lamplight, with a delicious touch of pink. Pert breasts flared at him behind the thin fabric of the tank top.

"That's all the clothes you brought?"

"That's all I need to sleep. I'm better dressed than you are." She glanced at Quinn's navy boxers and took a longer look at his naked upper body. "You certainly keep fit." They almost touched as their bodies crowded the tiny room. Then her boxers brushed against him as she turned around.

"This will do just fine for a bed." She laid the blanket on the couch and the pillow on the armrest. After checking her cell phone, she turned it off and laid it on the floor next to her room key and poncho.

Quinn looked at the cheap lock on the door, then picked up one of the metal chairs from the dinette table and leaned it so the top jammed under the doorknob. From his duffel bag, he withdrew two screw-locks, placed them on the windowsills and screwed them tight. He opened a zippered compartment and removed his 9mm and its holster. He checked the magazine, cocked the gun and put the safety on, and laid it within reach under his bed. After a moment's thought, he removed the spare magazine and laid it next to the 9mm.

"Why do you carry a gun? Is it loaded?" She sat cross-legged on the couch and watched him.

"For protection, and yes, so don't touch." There was no point in telling her what he'd learned about the ex-cons.

She looked around the room. "What is that metal pitcher on top of the hot plate?"

He sat on his bed. "It's an old-fashioned kind of coffee maker called a percolator. Makes pretty good coffee, if you like it strong."

"We must try it in the morning. Everything in this motel is so old-fashioned and funny. And what's that metal thing attached to the head of your bed? The one that says 'Magic Fingers'?"

"Another relic from the past. You put two quarters in the slots and it vibrates the bed for a few minutes. Sort of massages you."

She glanced at the pile of pocket change on his end table. Her eyes caught his, and she leaned forward, her tank top exposing the deepening "v" between her breasts. "Then we should certainly try that. You look a bit tense. It'll help us sleep."

23

She picked up two quarters from the pile of change and dropped them in the slots of the metal box, then sat next to Quinn on the bed.

A metallic hum filled the air as the bed gently vibrated.

"Oh! Doesn't that feel good?" She snuggled up against him.

"That does it." Quinn got up from the vibrating bed.

Why hadn't he known better than to buy her story and let her in? He grunted as he removed his gun and spare clip from under the bed and tucked them under the couch.

This was no time for her adolescent silliness. He had to get her safely through the night. He turned off the lamp next to the bed, and the small room plunged into darkness. The vinyl couch cushions were clammy as he lay down and pulled the thin blanket over him. "I'll take the couch. We won't need any help going to sleep. And speaking of sleep, it's time. Good night, Rebekah."

"Well, goodnight, then," Rebekah giggled as she pulled up the bed covers.

He lay on the couch, and she lay on the bed, both facing the front window. The bed stopped vibrating, and they listened in silence as rain beat on the roof and splashed against the glass.

With his gun by his side and the girl locked in his cabin, Quinn's small section of the universe now felt safe. Outside, lightning flashed in the distance and the thunder rumbled quietly. The storm was making its way west.

The falling rain finally soothed his soul. He turned on his side and fell asleep.

ONE HOUR *later*

THE MUFFLED SHOUT might have been part of a dream.

Quinn awakened with a start. He lay still on the couch, sorting out the sounds around him.

Across the room, Rebekah was asleep on the bed, making soft breathing noises.

Maybe the noise was just the falling rain. Its patter was like chanting voices huddled outside, warning about something. He focused his hearing and isolated the plop-plop of raindrops on puddles and the gurgle of an overflowing gutter.

His ears perked at the sharp sound of breaking glass.

He lifted his head and looked out the front window. His eyes adjusted and he made out the tall shapes of the palm trees and the outlines of the cabins. The scene was darker than before.

Rebekah's cabin porch light was off. Perhaps the old man had awoken and turned it off.

From somewhere outside came another muffled shout, and then a grunting noise, lower-pitched, from a different man's voice.

Quinn rolled off the couch and crouched below the window. He pressed his face near the glass, straining to see through the muted shades of black and gray.

The skin on the back of his neck crawled when he saw that the door to Rebekah's cabin was ajar. It moved in the wind, letting the rain inside. Her cabin was dark.

His stomach churned as he realized the Paradise's complete lack of security. Behind the cabins was a large asphalt parking lot, with a parking space behind each cabin. And beyond that? Vacant land, unfenced, leaving the complex wide open to intruders.

A shape to the right of her cabin caught his eye. Outlined by the slanting rain, it was black and square, about as wide as it was tall. The strange-looking form moved to the right, floating like some sort of phantasm toward the farthest cabin.

Quinn unscrewed the lock and slid the window sideways, opening it. Now footsteps crunched in the gravel outside. Whatever it was, it was not floating, and it had legs. A close examination revealed round contours at its top. The curves of human heads.

Below the heads were the curves of shoulders and torsos. The thing was two humans moving together. No, three. The two humans on the ends were carrying the smaller one in the middle. They moved as a group and headed directly toward the farthest cabin, the one at the bottom of the "U".

Quinn's eyes further adjusted, and he made out the dim outlines of arms and legs. The bodies of the humans on the ends looked familiar. The man in the middle was struggling and indistinct. He shouted something whose words were garbled by the roar of the storm.

But the voice was as unmistakable as it had been in the Paradise Lounge. The man in the middle was Dr. Hartman. He was pinned between Alpha and Street.

They were only steps from the cabin. Beyond it was parked a commercial van. The van that had "Coast Cities Auto Repair" on the sides.

They came for the girl.

Quinn's mind raced as he pulled on his jeans, tee-shirt and boots. The men broke into Rebekah's cabin and found she wasn't there. Did they find Rebekah's note? Then they knew where she was and would come for her. Were they taking Hartman hostage to get the girl?

He grabbed his phone. *Call 911. Get Hartman to safety. Hold the four men until the police come.*

The blank screen stared up at him. Was the damn thing dead? He pressed the power button, and the tiny light glowed in the center, signaling a boot-up.

Who'd turned his phone off? He always left it on. This wasted precious seconds. He watched the maddeningly slow process as the phone came to life.

A red light on his phone blinked, signaling urgent texts. Another light showed three missed calls. He frowned as he waited for the texts to download.

Where are you?

His phone vibrated as the next text came in.

URGENT CALL ASAP

The screen darkened as the signal dropped out. Quinn looked up, waiting for his phone to connect again. Muffled voices and a heavy thump cut through the sounds of the storm. He looked out the window to see the front door of Alpha's cabin open and the three men disappear into it.

His phone vibrated as more of Will's texts downloaded.

Hacked home computer of Alpha leader.

The girl stirred. She yawned and turned over. "What's going on?"

"Don't know yet. Did you turn off my phone?"

"Yes. It kept vibrating and waking me up. I didn't want it to wake you. I felt guilty about bothering you, so I turned it off so you could sleep. I always turn mine off when I go to bed, don't you?" She sat up in bed. "Is something wrong?"

Quinn broke into a cold sweat as his phone continued to buzz with each of Will's text updates.

All four men are jihadists. Homegrown. Radicalized while in prison.

Hiding in freaking plain sight. Terror attack planned.

The door to Alpha's cabin opened, and the silhouette of a man wearing a baseball cap emerged. Quinn's heart hammered as his phone vibrated with more texts.

Terror attack planned for San Francisco landmark.

Large quantities of explosives stored in Oakland warehouse.

Locations unknown.

Baseball-Cap stood guard in front of Alpha's cabin. He turned slightly, revealing the silhouette of a rifle with a circular, high-capacity drum magazine.

Quinn's phone vibrated as additional texts downloaded.

Indications attack may be imminent.

FBI and police alerted but with weather and distance ETA to your location two hours plus.

Apprehend and detain all four hostiles ASAP CONFIRM

CONFIRM

The "dammit" was left off. He was texting a reply when his phone vibrated with a phone call.

"Will, I'm on—"

Will cut him off. "Michael, can you see their cabin? Do you see a light?"

"A bright light just appeared in the side window. How did you—"

"We're scanning the whole damn motel. That's the video light from one of their phones. Hold on, I'm patching you in." There was a pause, and Quinn heard Will talking on another line, then he came back. "Check your screen."

A bright, color video feed filled Quinn's cell phone screen. Dr. Hartman stood in the corner of a room wearing a white tee-shirt, his hair in disarray and his face flushed red. His gray eyes stared at the camera with defiance. The sharp steel blade of a machete pressed against his throat.

Alpha stood behind Hartman, his beefy arm wrapped around the professor's neck and his hand firmly gripping the machete. Alpha was speaking to the camera. Blood dripped from his right cheek, and there were several small cuts as if a piece of broken glass had been scraped down it. Dr. Hartman had fought back.

"Michael, we picked up their conversation. They're on their way to Oakland to pick up the explosives for their San Francisco attack. Damn these bastards, they're talking about taking out hundreds of civilians. They've been planning this attack since they were in prison. Folsom is a hotbed of this jailhouse jihadist garbage." Will took a breath and lowered his voice. "Their target right now, though, is Dr. Hartman."

"Why are they after Hartman?"

"They're going to execute him as an infidel. It's a freaking crime of opportunity, Michael. They found out who Hartman was, and that he's world-famous, from that television newscast in the lounge. By killing him, they can send a shock wave around the globe and make themselves known before their big event."

"And the girl?" Quinn glanced across the room. Rebekah sat upright on the edge of the bed, listening to every word. Her eyes were wide with fear and her knees shook.

"She's just a bonus to them. She's entertainment. When they saw Hartman leave her alone with you, they figured all they had to do was get rid of you and they would have the girl all to themselves after they got rid of Hartman.

"Right now, the leader is giving a speech to the camera. When he's done, they're going to behead Hartman, then upload the damn video for the whole world to see."

Will paused, and Quinn sensed controlled fury in his voice when he spoke again. "Neutralize them, Michael. Any means necessary,"

"Copy, out." Quinn tucked the phone into his back pocket.

"What are—" Rebekah went silent as he raised his hand.

He tucked his 9mm into his waist holster and put the spare magazine in his pocket. He reached into the back of the duffel bag to a zippered compartment, withdrew his suppressor, and screwed it into the barrel of his 9mm. Next, he removed an innocent-looking pouch which contained an M67 hand grenade and clipped the small pouch to his belt.

"Stay here and keep the door locked. I'll be back." He looked around the room at the rectangular window above the couch. It faced away from the front of the cabin and appeared big enough to crawl through. He climbed onto the couch, unscrewed the lock, and slid the window sideways, opening it. Next, he popped out the screen and laid it on the couch. One leg on top of the couch and the other on the windowsill, he climbed through, perched on the sill, and jumped.

He landed in muddy grass. Wind whistled around him and chilly rain pelted his hair and skin. Ignoring his soaked clothing, he crouched and peered around the corner rain-gutter. Baseball-Cap stood guard in front of the men's cabin, his rifle at the ready.

Quinn drew his 9mm. He had seconds, maybe a minute, before they executed Hartman. He scooped up a handful of wet rocks and put them in his pocket. His plan, though rough, was complete by the time he aimed his 9mm.

Say goodbye to freaking Baseball-Cap.

The 9mm spat three times. The silhouette of Baseball-Cap twitched like a marionette, then crumpled to the wet ground.

Quinn was already running through the grass toward the men's cabin. He'd gambled that the noise inside their cabin, plus the noise from the storm, would drown out his gunfire and movement. No one came out the front door to see what had happened to Baseball-Cap.

Now to stop the execution.

The cell phone video had shown Hartman in a rear corner of the room, with Alpha holding the machete to his throat. Quinn ran past Baseball Cap's body to the side of the cabin, stopped and aimed through the side window at the bright light in the opposite corner of the room. He fired four shots, hoping to hit the head and torso of the cameraman.

The window shattered and the light bobbed crazily, then went dark. Shouts rang out.

The tip of a rifle barrel poked out of the window and knocked out the remaining window glass. Quinn holstered his gun and sprinted the short distance to the back of the cabin. A burst of automatic fire thumped the ground behind him, another nipped at his heels, and then he made a running leap to the top of the grey metal power meter adjacent to the rear corner of the cabin.

He landed with both feet on top of the rain-slicked meter and leaped straight up toward the cabin roof. The three-foot-tall meter gave him just enough of a boost to grab the edges of the shake shingles. A piece of a wet wood shingle broke off in one hand, but the rest held, and he hauled himself up and onto the steeply pitched roof.

He crouched on all fours, trying to distribute his weight evenly and be as light as possible. The winds tore at him and rain slammed into his face, but his fingers found a firm grip on the rough edges of the wet shingles. He crept his way along the roof peak, up to the front of the cabin. Shouts and curses poured through the broken window below him. The men inside were arguing about what to do next.

Quinn straddled the roof peak, drew his 9mm, and peered over the front edge. With the camera light out, everything had plunged back into darkness. Baseball-Cap's corpse lay in a heap in front of the door, raindrops glancing off of his body and into muddy puddles.

Quinn grabbed the rocks from his pocket and tossed them against the outside wall above the side window. A rifle barrel poked out and sprayed automatic fire. At the same time, the front door opened and another rifle barrel appeared, firing side-to-side.

The head and shoulders of Meth cautiously leaned out of the doorway, and his rifle spat longer bursts.

Quinn fired two shots directly onto the top of Meth's head. Dark mist sprayed in all directions and Meth fell forward, dropping his rifle as he collapsed over Baseball-Cap's body. He landed face down on the wet ground and lay still.

Two down, two to go. Quinn removed his empty clip and inserted his only spare. He would have to conserve ammo.

The world exploded around him.

Quinn sprang up into the air as blasts of rifle fire echoed on all sides. Pieces of wood and drywall ricocheted off him and flew in all directions as the gunmen inside raked the entire roof, side to side, and then front and back, with dozens of rounds. Twisting his body to avoid the fusillade, he came down at an awkward angle on the slippery edge of the roof and half-jumped, half-fell to the ground on the side of the cabin.

He landed hard in the wet grass and rolled. Pain shot up his left ankle, and his thigh burned. But he lay in darkness at an angle where he would be difficult to spot in the rain. He spat mud out of his mouth and aimed his 9mm with both hands at the front entrance. His bare arms shivered in the cold. He took a deep breath and focused on keeping them still.

The front door opened, and rifle fire blasted the entire area in front of the house. Quinn watched as three men exited the front door. Alpha was in front, the machete in a sheath strapped to his thigh, and Street was in back. They held Hartman, who seemed to have gone limp, tightly between them, and Alpha and Street each cradled a rifle in their outside arm. They fired staccato bursts as they stepped around the bodies of Meth and Baseball Cap and made for the parking lot behind the cabin.

Quinn couldn't get a clear shot. The receding target became a black blob in the darkness, and their cover fire kept him from moving closer. He rolled against the muddy outside of the cabin to minimize his visibility.

They headed toward the van, which was parked facing away from the cabin. He moved his 9mm back and forth as they made their way, looking for a shot, but it was hopeless. All he could do was watch. If they got away, Hartman was a dead man.

Alpha shouted something at Street, who paused firing and reached in his coverall pocket, removed a small object, and pointed it at the van.

The van's taillights and headlights blinked on. The headlights shone on the empty parking lot. The red taillights, though dimmer than the headlights, produced enough pale, blood-red illumination to clearly reveal Quinn lying on the ground against the cabin. Raindrops splattered red in puddles around him.

"I got the bastard," shouted Street's black shape.

Street raised his rifle and aimed it at Quinn. As he raised the rifle he let go of Dr. Hartman.

The black shape of Dr. Hartman had been still. Now he sprang to life, twisting out of Alpha's grasp and giving Street a violent shove sideways.

Street stumbled three, four steps away from the other two. His silhouette was now separate from the others. Quinn fired three shots at the torso and head. Street yelled as the bullets hit. His rifle slipped out of his hands and splashed in a puddle. He slumped sideways, then fell to the ground and lay still.

Alpha screamed curses and blasted rifle fire in Quinn's direction. He grabbed Dr. Hartman in a headlock and dragged him toward the van, laying a steady stream of cover fire as he went.

Bullets splattered in the mud and thudded into the cabin wall behind Quinn. He rolled out of the pool of red light and into darkness, aiming his 9mm. The moving target was too indistinct and too far away.

The black form of Alpha holding Hartman moved in an arc away from him and toward the front of the van. Their path meant he would never have a clear shot at Alpha.

Quinn felt for the pouch and removed the grenade. He pulled himself into a crouch and estimated the distance to the van.

He grabbed the grenade's pull-ring with his index finger, twisted it, and ripped it out. One more look at the distance, and he used a side throw to lob the grenade. The grenade bounced once on the asphalt and rolled under the van.

The explosion lifted the van completely off the ground and sent orange and yellow flames high into the air. When Quinn lifted his head he saw massive smoke clouds billowing into the night and burning wreckage everywhere, the fires blazing fiercely despite the rain.

Alpha, still holding Dr. Hartman in a headlock, stopped and faced the inferno. Both men had their backs to Quinn. Alpha dropped the rifle he'd been carrying and unsheathed the machete strapped to his thigh.

Now.

Quinn sprang to his feet and sprinted forward. Alpha lifted his machete high in the air and shouted something. The machete was still pointing at the sky when Quinn got within range, dropped to one knee, and fired three shots at Alpha's head and upper body.

Alpha's shout became a bloodcurdling scream that echoed in the surrounding hills. His black silhouette dropped the machete. It took one heavy step forward, then toppled to the ground, still.

Dawn

"The police, coroner, and FBI have all left... ...No, just the girl and me now... She's asleep, gave her a sedative... Yes, I'll tell her."

Quinn leaned against the front porch of his cabin, a mug of black coffee in one hand, his cell phone in the other.

As he spoke, he watched the long night surrender to daybreak. Raindrops glistened on the wet grass around him. The cool morning air had the earthy scent that lingers after a storm has moved on.

"I'm fine. The back of the cabin absorbed most of the shrapnel. Flesh wound in the leg, twisted ankle. That's all. Paramedics patched me up... Of course not... Two hours or so... Thank you, sir... Copy, out."

He put his phone in his pocket and sipped the dark coffee, watching the golden sun peek over rolling green hills.

Footsteps sounded behind him.

The girl, wrapped in the thin blanket and holding a mug of coffee, walked barefoot onto the porch. Her face was pale. He gave her a reassuring smile.

"Good morning, Rebekah. I've got some good news. Dr. Hartman will be released from the hospital later today. Just cuts and bruises. Quite the stamina that man has. Says he will join you at Stanford in a day or two." Quinn watched her expression brighten. "And how is your first cup of percolator coffee?"

"With that news, it's the best coffee I've ever had."

She looked to her right. A broad circle of yellow tape surrounded a crime scene that, with its charred ground and piles of ashes and blasted remnants of the van, looked like something from an apocalypse.

Her voice grew somber. "I don't know how to say this, but after what happened, I keep thinking about evil people and the horrible things they do. I've read about them in news reports, of course, but they were always so far away. Evil was just an abstraction to me. Last night was the first time I've seen it first-hand. Now it's so real. What will stop it?"

"Whatever it takes."

"I thought you might say something like that." She turned away from the crime scene and looked at him. "And where are you headed?"

"South on PCH. Duty calls." He motioned to the duffel bag at his feet.

"We're going in opposite directions, then. I was hoping we could spend a bit more time together. Well, I guess this is goodbye." She extended her hand.

Quinn grasped the tender hand he'd first touched just the night before. A weight seemed to lift off his shoulders.

"Let's calendar in another time then, Rebekah. We should get better acquainted."

Her eyebrows raised in an are-you-serious look. "Well, you could visit me at Stanford, when you're up that way."

"Only if you let me take you to dinner at Te Amo."

"And that is?"

"My favorite Italian restaurant in the area. And you can tell me all about your passion over a bottle of Chianti." He picked up his duffel bag.

"My passion?"

"Your doctoral thesis, of course. I believe it is on the Riemann Hypothesis? You started to tell me about it last night. But, we got a bit distracted."

A breeze ruffled the girl's hair and lifted her blanket. She was still clad in her rumpled boxer shorts and cotton tank top. Goosebumps showed on the white curves of her slender ballerina's body. It was even more beautiful in the light of day.

She demurely put a hand between her legs, pulling the blanket back in place.

The corners of her lips turned up in a smile. "Michael, do you really want to hear about that?"

"Well, to start."

Reviews for the international best-seller Michael Quinn novel *Night of the Bonfire*:

"Five stars, worthy of ten... grabs your attention and takes you for a wild ride!" - Goodreads review

"This appealing spy... is ready for his own series." - Kirkus review

"Had me holding my breath and tensing with suspense... can't wait for more." - Amazon review

FOR MORE WORKS BY THE AUTHOR, VISIT WWW.KEVINSCOTTOLSON.COM

58250909R00022

Made in the USA
Middletown, DE
05 August 2019